Officer Toothbrush, Smileytooth, and Officer Toothpaste are good friends.

Together they fight cavities that try to hurt Smileytooth and other teeth.

Smileytooth lives on Gum Street
with all of his tooth friends.

One day Officer Toothpaste and Officer Toothbrush drove down Gum Street in their special police car to visit Smileytooth.

They were also on the lookout for Plaque and his Cavity Gang. Plaque and his Gang hurt teeth by making holes in them called cavities.

Suddenly, they saw Smileytooth wildly waving at them and pointing down the street.

The police car screeched to a stop, and Officer Toothbrush rolled down the window and asked,

"What's the matter, Smileytooth?"

Smileytooth yelled, "I just saw Plaque and his Gang sneaking around the corner and getting ready to hurt a tooth!"

"OK, we'll catch them," Officer Toothpaste said. Then the officers drove away fast!

The officers stopped the police car near the curve of Gum Street, climbed out, and sneaked around the corner.

The officers were searching around one tooth when they spotted Plaque starting to make a hole in the next tooth.

Then Officer Toothbrush and Officer Toothpaste chased Plaque up and down Gum Street.

Luckily, they were too fast for Plaque.

Officer Toothbrush grabbed him by the arm, while Officer Toothpaste tackled him.

Then the officers slapped handcuffs on Plaque's wrists and hauled him away to jail.

When Officer Toothbrush and Officer Toothpaste returned, they brushed all the teeth very well to make sure that all were rid of Plaque's gang members.

Finally, the whole Cavity Gang was washed away.

That afternoon the dentist looked at all of the teeth on Gum Street.

He was pleased to see that they were shiny and clean.

Then he said, "Brush every day after meals, and you will always have clean and shiny teeth."

Smileytooth was very happy. Now all of his friends were shiny and clean just as he was.

And you, too, can be like Smileytooth and his friends if you brush your teeth every day just as the dentist tells you to.